Red = stop,
yellow = caution,
green = go.

Flagger ahead.

Workers present.

Pay attention.
You might need to stop.

No! This is the wrong
way to go!

Look both ways
before crossing.
Don't walk when the
red hand is up!

Yes! You can park here.

There's a
fire station here.

Here's a lane for
bikers only.

Must turn right!

Sorry, but you'll have to
go a different way.

A place to go for
information or help.

Slow down for
tricky turn ahead.

RUNAWAY SIGNS

JOAN HOLUB

ALISON FARRELL

Nancy Paulsen Books

Day in and day out, the two kids on the School Crossing sign showed the students where to cross safely.

It was an important job.

Still, on the last day of school, the stick girl and stick boy on the School Crossing sign couldn't help but feel left out as the students headed off on their vacations.

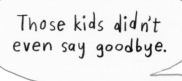

The sign kids soon found another
sign who wanted to explore.

And so the three of them traveled out into the world, seeking adventure.

Along the way, they met more signs doing important jobs.

Lots of signs jumped at the chance to take a vacation.

And soon they discovered the perfect place
for fun and adventure.

Adventureland turned out to be great.
The signs were having a whale of a good time.

But then the signs noticed that something wasn't right.

With the signs gone, the town was in a tangle.

OKAY, SIGNS!

STOP!

The party's OVER!

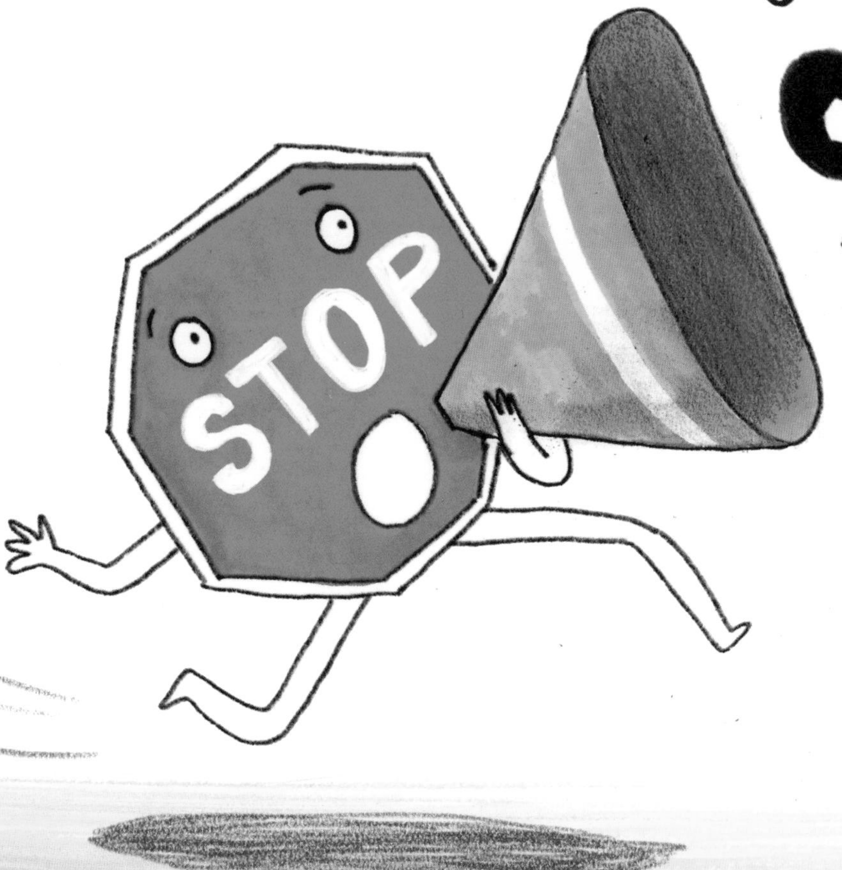

It was time to get back to work.

The signs raced back to their posts.

Back in town, they took their usual places.

All the people in town were so appreciative to have things back to normal.

The signs felt so good, they decided they'd never leave their posts again.

Well, almost never.

For Nancy Paulsen—J.H.

To Finn—A.F.

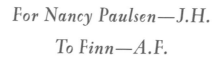

NANCY PAULSEN BOOKS

An imprint of Penguin Random House LLC, New York

Text copyright © 2020 by Joan Holub | Illustrations copyright © 2020 by Alison Farrell | Penguin supports copyright. Copyright fuels creativity, encourages diverse voices, promotes free speech, and creates a vibrant culture. Thank you for buying an authorized edition of this book and for complying with copyright laws by not reproducing, scanning, or distributing any part of it in any form without permission. You are supporting writers and allowing Penguin to continue to publish books for every reader.

Nancy Paulsen Books is a trademark of Penguin Random House LLC.

Visit us online at penguinrandomhouse.com

Library of Congress Cataloging-in-Publication Data
Names: Holub, Joan, author. | Farrell, Alison, 1979– illustrator. | Title: Runaway signs / Joan Holub; illustrated by Alison Farrell. | Description: New York: Nancy Paulsen Books, [2020] | Summary: When all of the signs except Caution, from School Crossing to Ranger Station to a stoplight, decide to take a vacation, they learn how important their jobs really are. | Identifiers: LCCN 2019018207 | ISBN 9780399172250 (hardcover: alk. paper) | ISBN 9780698197626 (ebook) | ISBN 9780698197619 (ebook) | Subjects: | CYAC: Street signs—Fiction. | Traffic signs and signals—Fiction. | Signs and signboards—Fiction. | Humorous stories. Classification: LCC PZ7.H7427 Run 2020 | DDC [E]—dc23 LC record available at https://lccn.loc.gov/2019018207

Manufactured in China by RR Donnelley Asia Printing Solutions Ltd.
ISBN 9780399172250
1 3 5 7 9 10 8 6 4 2
Design by Eileen Savage | Text set in Oneleigh OT
The illustrations were done in gouache and ink.

School crossing.

When you see this sign, STOP!

Like to read? Here's a library.

Watch out! Cows may cross here. Moo!

GRRROWL! Look out for bears.

Be prepared to stop for merging traffic.

Make way for ducks. Quack.

Don't go faster than 20 miles an hour.

Wheelchair accessible.

Hooray! A hiking trail.

Sorry!

Watch out!

Road only goes one way.

31901066136005